THE TROUBLE WITH FUN

Check out my stellar Guide to Space Station Slang on page 82!

BY **MARILYN SADLER**
ILLUSTRATED BY **ROGER BOLLEN**

A Stepping Stone Book™

Random House 🏠 New York

Text copyright © 2001 by Marilyn Sadler
Illustrations copyright © 2001 by Roger Bollen
Published in the United States by Random House, Inc., New York, and
simultaneously in Canada by Random House of Canada Limited, Toronto.

www.randomhouse.com/kids

Library of Congress Cataloging-in-Publication Data
Sadler, Marilyn.   The trouble with fun / by Marilyn Sadler ; illustrated by Roger Bollen.
p.   cm.
"Zenon, girl of the 21st century, book #3."
"A stepping stone book."
SUMMARY: A twenty-first-century girl living on a space station agrees to entertain
the daughter of an important Earth scientist, but the visitor's idea of fun
could mean big trouble for Zenon.
ISBN 0-679-89251-6 (trade) — ISBN 0-679-99251-0 (lib. bdg.)
[1. Behavior—Fiction.   2. Hospitality—Fiction.   3. Space stations—Fiction.
4. Science fiction.]
I. Bollen, Roger, ill.   II. Title.   PZ7.S1239   Tr 2001   [Fic]—dc21   2001041760

Printed in the United States of America   November 2001   10 9 8 7 6 5 4 3 2 1

CONTENTS

1
VISITORS FROM EARTH

"Hurry up, Zenon! The shuttle from Earth will be landing in forty-six minutes!" shouted my dad.

I rolled out of bed and stared at myself in the bathroom mirror. I looked like a Blotozoid Zombie.

"I'm coming, Dad!" I shouted back, splashing cold water on my face.

Sometimes my dad fully shivered me out. He had been going lunar over his Fuddle-Frisson project for as long as I could remember. It was one of the reasons we had moved to Space Station 9 almost ten years earlier.

"The future is in Fuddle-Frisson, honey," he used to tell me.

I didn't see what was so thermo about Fuddle-Frisson myself. Something was always going wrong. If it wasn't flystrom trouble, it was problems with the tutons.

At least now, after all these years, help was on the way. It was arriving in forty-six minutes on a space shuttle from Earth.

"Morning glorious!" I said, sliding into my seat at the kitchen table. "What's for breakfast?"

Mom kissed me on top of my head. Then she turned toward Woma.

Woma was our robotic maid. Without her, there would be no breakfast.

"Pandorian toast with sliced whambamas," she said, smiling down at me.

Woma made the best Pandorian toast in the galaxy.

"Stellar!" I said as she placed my breakfast in front of me.

I was chewing my last bite of Pandorian toast when my dad's data-pad alarm went off.

"Time to blast off!" he shouted, jumping up from the table. "The shuttle will be landing in eighteen minutes!"

The next thing I knew, Dad was moving us out the door and down the hallway. We reached the Wait Platform just as the Z-Train pulled up.

"Space shuttle port, please!" Dad announced as we boarded.

"Very good, sir," answered Drovo, the train's robotic driver.

I sat down behind my parents. We traveled down the tunnel, and I looked out the window. When we stopped at the next Wait Platform, more people stepped on board. One of them was my best friend, Nebula.

"Ceedus-Lupeedus!" I shouted. "Where are you going, Neb?"

Nebula sat down in the seat next to me. She had the wild-eyed look of a Lootar. I knew at once where she was going—shopping.

"I need a new Nan Kloddy jacket," she said.

Then she noticed my parents.

"Where are *you* going?" she asked, looking at me curiously.

"We're going to the space shuttle port to pick up a famous scientist from Earth," I said. "He's going to help my dad with his Fuddle-Frisson project."

I could always tell what Neb was thinking. I guess that's why she's my best friend. Right then, she was wondering why *I* was going to the shuttle port. After all, the scientist from Earth was coming to see my dad, not *me*.

"The scientist is bringing his daughter," I explained. "She's staying with me for as long as he's here."

A look of horror spread across Neb's face.

"How *inky*!" she said. "An *alien*!"

Neb had a way of going supernova over nothing.

"She's from *Earth*, Neb! Not the outer rim of the *Fenebula*!" I said.

Before Neb had a chance to go into global meltdown, the train came to a stop at the Big Wheel Shopping Mall. Nebula jumped out of her seat and disappeared down the aisle.

To tell you the truth, I was happy to see Neb go. Just thinking about the girl from Earth gave me geezle bumps.

What if I didn't like her? I worried.

I didn't need Neb to shiver me out more.

When we arrived at the space shuttle port, it was crowded with people. We found some seats and sat down.

"The shuttle is due to arrive in two minutes," said my dad, smiling.

It was thermo to see Dad so happy. He hadn't been this excited since the Quantum Comets beat the Earth Astros in the spaceball championship.

Exactly two minutes later, just like my dad said, the shuttle from Earth landed. Then the door of the shuttle opened and the famous Earth scientist stepped out. He was carrying a Laser Frissonometer.

"There he is, Zenon," said my dad. "The famous Harold Wiggins—in the flesh!"

My dad and mom hurried over to greet him.

Me, I stood frozen in place.

In the shuttle doorway stood Harold Wiggins's daughter.

Her hair was the color of a Pandorian sunrise. Her clothes sparkled like a solar mist. And she was as skinny as a Blotozoid Freefron.

2
THE NECKLACE

Harold Wiggins's daughter raced down the shuttle stairway and over to me. She was grinning from ear to ear.

"I'm Teena Wiggins!" she cried, shaking my hand. "You must be Zenon Kar!"

I was surprised to learn that Teena knew all about me.

She knew my best friend's name was Nebula. She knew my favorite music group was Microbe. She even knew I played spaceball.

"I looked you up on my data pad!" she said. "You're stellar, Zenon Kar!"

It was going to be hard not to like Teena Wiggins.

Dad showed Teena and her father to the train. Teena talked to my parents all the way home. She asked my mom about life on the space station. Then she called my dad the "Father of Fuddle-Frisson."

By the time we got home, my parents liked Teena, too.

When we walked in the door, Bobo, my robotic dog, floated up to greet us.

Teena dropped her suitcase and gathered Bobo up in her arms. She had never seen a robotic dog before.

"What a cute puppy!" she cried, hugging him.

Needless to say, Bobo also liked Teena. After that, he stuck to her like a tuton to a kryzon.

That night, Woma fixed beet loaf and mashed potatoes for dinner. Teena and her father could not stop talking about how delicious it was. When Woma served the Whambama Splits for dessert, they went quasar.

After dinner, my parents and Mr. Wiggins sat down in the living room to talk. Teena and I went to my room. I showed her where to put her things. Then I helped her unpack.

Teena had clothes I had never seen before. They were made from materials that sparkled and glowed. Sometimes they even changed colors.

"These are so stellar!" I said, hanging them up in my closet.

I didn't know anything about Earth. I was born there. But I was a baby when we left to live on the space station. Everything about it was alien to me.

"What kind of music do you listen to down there?" I asked.

Teena dug through her suitcase and pulled out a 3D-CD.

"This is my favorite group!" she said. "It's an all-girl band called Earth Angels!"

Teena played her 3D-CD for me and we danced. She showed me how everyone was dancing on Earth.

I'll have to show these new moves to Nebula, I thought as I spun around my room.

After a while, I couldn't dance any longer.
I stretched out on my bed to cool my boosters.

Teena didn't seem tired at all. She just
kept dancing.

For the first time, I noticed the necklace
swinging from Teena's neck. Like everything
else of hers, it was stellar.

"I love your necklace!" I told her.

"Oh, it isn't really a necklace," said Teena,
bobbing up and down to the music. "It's an
Alfred Geezle–designed Mini Motion-Picture
Camera."

Teena stopped dancing for a minute and
took off her necklace. Then she leaned over
and fastened it around my neck.

"I film my classes in school so that I don't have to pay attention," she explained.

I looked down at Teena's necklace. Up close, I could see that it was a camera. But, Ceedus-Lupeedus, I couldn't wear it to school!

"Mr. Peres would go lunar!" I cried.

"That's the stellar thing about Alfred Geezle's design!" said Teena. "Mr. Peres will never know!"

That night, I fell asleep with Teena's Mini Motion-Picture Camera around my neck.

It was true that everything about Teena was alien. But like I would tell my best friend, Neb, it was a *good* kind of alien.

3
STELLAR BEYOND BELIEF

The next morning, Teena and I could not get out of bed. I guess we shouldn't have stayed up so late. But we were having so much fun!

Mom, Dad, and Woma all took turns trying to wake us.

"You're going to be late for school!" they said.

Finally, with my mind in a Martian mist, I rolled out of bed.

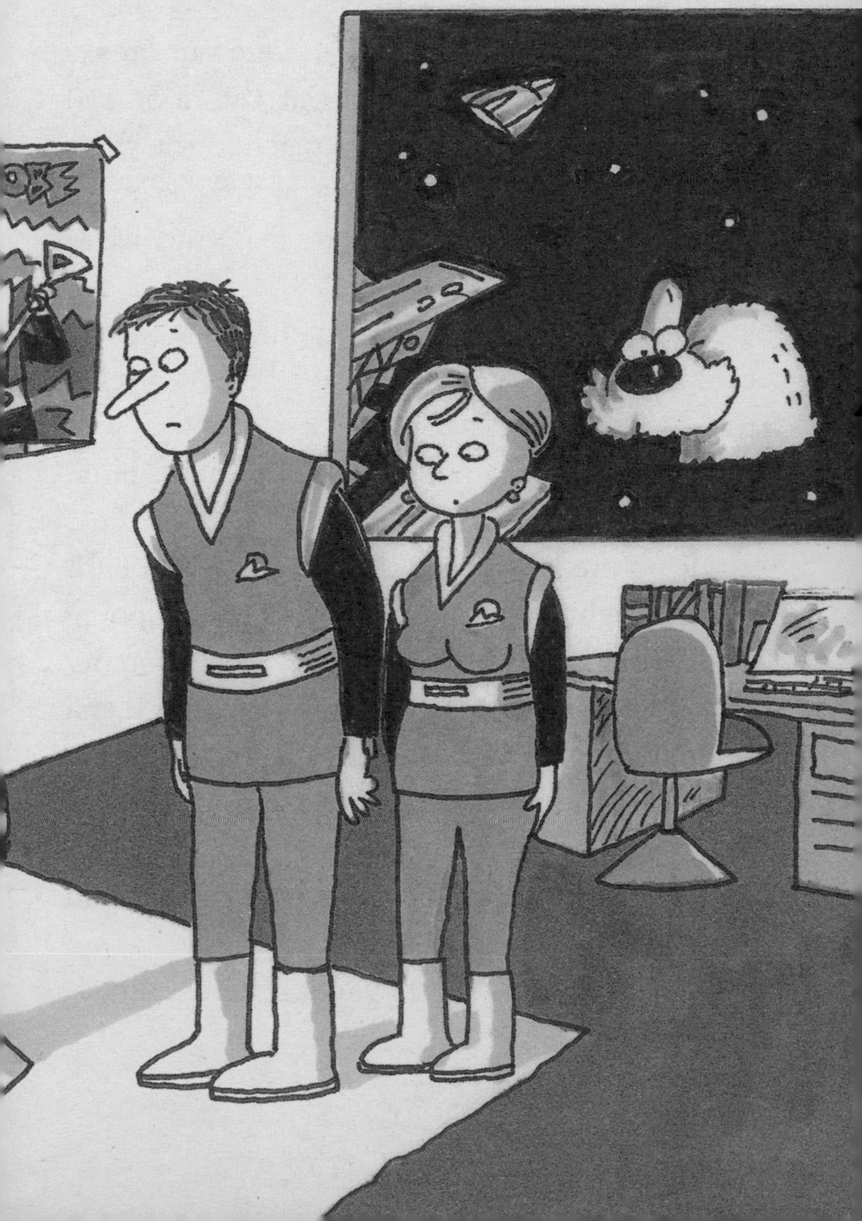

"Morning glorious, Teena," I whispered, shaking her.

Teena and I got dressed and ate our breakfasts in a hurry. We dashed out the door and down the hallway. When we reached the Wait Platform, the Q-Train was just pulling away.

"Ceedus-Lupeedus!" I cried. "Now we're *really* going to be late!"

Teena wasn't flared-up at all. She was as cool as a Milky Way Float. So I began to relax too.

The next train pulled up ten minutes later, and we were on our way.

I pointed out all the places I thought Teena might like: the Big Wheel Shopping Mall, the Laser Beam Arcade, the Mercury Music Store, and the Mars Malt. Teena wanted to go to all of them.

Then the train finally stopped in front of my school.

"This is Quantum Elementary!" I said proudly.

Mr. Peres was in the middle of a Fuddlenomics lesson when we walked into my classroom.

I was just about to introduce him to Teena when Teena beat me to it.

"Morning glorious, Mr. Peres!" she cried, shaking his hand. "My name is Teena Wiggins! It is *so* thermo to meet you!"

Mr. Peres studied Teena's hair and clothes while he shook her hand. I could tell that he didn't know whether to go quasar or lunar.

"I am a guest of Zenon's," Teena said. "I just arrived this morning from Earth . . . which is why Zenon and I are late."

For a moment, I thought I didn't hear Teena correctly. *Did she say she arrived this morning?* I asked myself. I could not imagine that Teena would lie. But then I saw Mr. Peres's reaction.

"Oh, well, that's fine!" he said. "We always enjoy having visitors from Earth on Space Station 9!" Then he smiled at Teena and told her, "Please, take this seat in the front row."

It did not take Teena long to join in the Fuddlenomics lesson. Every time Mr. Peres asked a question, Teena's hand shot up. Teena knew more about Fuddlenomics than I did—and my dad was the "Father of Fuddle-Frisson."

When the bell finally rang for lunch, I was ready to blast out of there.

"I can't *wait* to meet your friends!" said Teena as we headed toward the cafeteria.

This was the moment I had been worried about. My friends could be pretty inky. If they didn't like you, they could really shiver you out.

When we got to the cafeteria, my friends were waiting for us.

Tad and Var had unhappy looks on their faces. Nebula looked downright scorchy.

I should have known better than to worry, though.

"You must be Nebula!" I heard Teena shout from behind me.

Teena ran up to Neb and threw her arms around her.

"I feel like I know you," she said. "Zenon has told me so much about you!"

Then Teena spotted Var.

"What a stellar outfit!" she cried, clasping her hands together. "It must be Nan Kloddy!"

And lastly, Teena turned to Tad.

"I read all about your Science Award!" she exclaimed. "Everyone on Earth is talking about you!"

I looked at my friends. They were grinning like Plutar Blanchies.

This isn't going to be so scorchy after all, I thought with relief.

I followed Teena and my friends into the cafeteria. We picked up our food trays and sat down. Then I ate my beetburger while they talked and talked.

On the way back to class, Neb leaned over and whispered in my ear, "Teena is stellar beyond belief, Zee!"

4
JOYRIDE

All in all, it had been a pretty thermo day. Mr. Peres thought Teena was a fine student, and my friends thought she was the most stellar girl in the universe.

I could finally relax and cool my boosters.

When the last bell rang, I was ready to blast off.

"Thank you, Mr. Peres!" I heard Teena say as we left the classroom. "Your class was super!"

When Teena and I got home from school, Woma greeted us with a plate of cookies.

"Have a Jupiter Snap!" I said to Teena.

Teena and I settled down to eat our cookies and talk about school. But before we could get started, the door buzzer sounded.

"Your friends are here!" said Woma, stepping aside to make way for Tad, Neb, and Var.

I was surprised to see them so soon. We'd only just left school.

"What's blasting?" I asked, passing them the plate of cookies.

"We thought we'd see what you two were doing," said Tad, sitting down next to Teena.

Neb and Var helped themselves to some cookies. Then they sat down, too.

"What do you do for fun on Earth, Teena?" asked Tad, biting into a Jupiter Snap.

Tad was born on the space station and had never spent much time on Earth.

"I hang out with my friends at a kids' club called Ground Hogs," said Teena. "We like to drink sodas and eat hot dogs."

"Ceedus-Lupeedus!" said Var. "I've never had a hot dog! We don't eat meat on the space station."

My friends and I were quiet for a minute. We were all thinking about eating meat. Then Nebula had a thermo idea.

"Let's take Teena to the Mars Malt!" she said. "She can see where *we* hang out!"

Teena jumped out of her seat.

"That's a stellar idea!" she shouted.

My friends and I jumped up, too. We went to the Mars Malt every day. But Teena made it seem like the most thermo thing to do in the universe.

On our way out the door, Teena spotted my hoverboard.

"Oh, Zee!" she cried. "Let's ride double to the Mars Malt!"

There were many things we weren't allowed to do with hoverboards on the space station. Riding double was one of them.

I was just about to explain the rules to Teena when she grabbed my hand. She pulled me onto my hoverboard. Then she took off down the hall like a comet on fire.

My friends were left behind as Teena shifted into hyperspeed.

Ceedus-Lupeedus! I thought. *We are really flying! I didn't know my Hyperspeed 100 could fly this fast!*

I was going quasar with excitement!

Then, all of a sudden, a big man appeared out of nowhere.

Teena made a quick turn and just missed hitting him. But we spun out of control, rolling over and over, bouncing off the space station wall.

Teena and I lay on the floor in a heap. When I looked up, my heart started pounding.

Captain Plank was staring down at us.

5
STARRY, STARRY NIGHT

I jumped up from the floor, full of apologies.

"I am *so* sorry, Captain Plank!" I said, picking up my hoverboard. "It will never happen again! I promise!"

Captain Plank frowned at us. He looked more flared-up than I had ever seen him.

Teena did not seem to notice.

"Captain Plank!" she shouted eagerly. "I have *always* wanted to meet you!"

Teena explained who she was and why she was on the space station. She did not act like someone who had nearly hit the captain of Space Station 9 with a hoverboard.

"You are the most stellar captain in the galaxy!" I heard her say as I quietly crept away.

Neb, Tad, and Var were standing at a distance. I hurried over to join them.

We watched as a big smile spread across Captain Plank's face. Then he patted Teena's head and disappeared down the hall of the space station.

I was truly impressed.

So were my friends.

"I wish I could pull that off," said Tad.

"Me too," said Var and Neb together.

I nodded in agreement. We all wanted to be like Teena.

After that, we went to the Mars Malt and ordered Whambama Shakes. Teena and my friends talked and laughed about how she'd gotten out of trouble today. First with Mr. Peres and then with Captain Plank.

"What do you want to do now?" I asked, sipping up the last of my shake.

Teena's eyes lit up like the moons of Jupiter.

"I have an idea!" she shouted, jumping up from her seat. "Come with me!"

My friends and I followed Teena down the hall. When we reached the end of it, Teena turned left toward Sector 7.

My friends and I stopped in our tracks. We looked at each other in surprise.

"We're not allowed to go down there, Teena!" I called after her.

Sector 7 held the exit deck for space-walking. I went quasar just thinking about it. I had always wanted to spacewalk. But the space station rules were very strict. My friends and I were not old enough.

"Come on!" shouted Teena. "Don't be such Blanchies!"

I knew my friends wanted to spacewalk as much as I did. We all stood in silence as we watched Teena disappear down the hall.

It seemed like we were all thinking the same thing: We wanted to be like Teena. And this was our chance.

Without waiting another moment, we bolted down the hall after her!

I knew what we were about to do was scorchy. But, *Ceedus-Lupeedus*, it was going to be fun!

The door to the exit deck was locked. So Teena pulled a small black box out of her backpack.

"What in the name of Neptune is *that*?" I asked.

"It's a special tool that unlocks any lock," said Teena. "My dad invented it. You might say I *borrowed* it from his lab."

Teena placed the small black box up against the door. The box made a series of clicking sounds. Then the door swung open.

We walked onto the exit deck, quickly shutting the door behind us.

On the wall hung space suits in many different sizes. We took some down and put them on in a hurry. Then we slipped the helmets over our heads.

Teena punched the controls on the door that led to outer space. I watched as the door slowly opened.

I took a deep breath. I was shaking like a Freefron.

My friends and I had tied ourselves together like a string of ornaments. One at a time, each of us stepped out of the door and fell into space.

Slowly we drifted away from the space station and toward the stars.

It was the most stellar-glorious moment of my life!

6
THE TANGLED TETHER

I floated quietly.

The stars sparkled all around me. I felt like I could reach out and touch them. But I knew they were light-years away.

I could not tell whether I was up . . . or down. I spun around slowly in all directions.

I wondered what my friends were thinking. They looked lunar, bobbing up and down against the stars. I wished I could talk to them. But then again, I liked the silence.

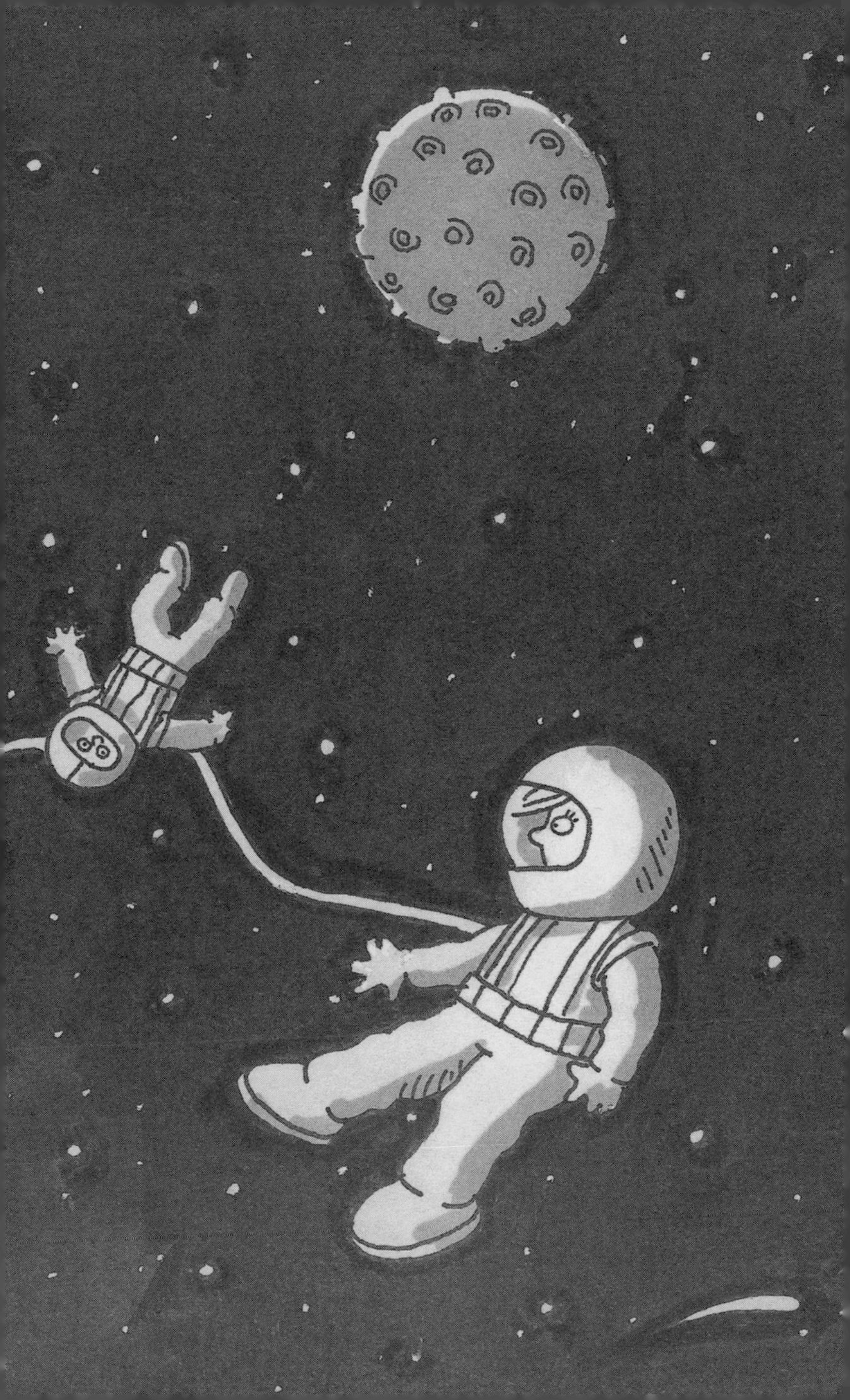

As I drifted about, my mind fell into a Martian mist. I felt peaceful and happy.

Then, all of a sudden, I snapped awake!

My tether line had gotten tangled around my leg. It was pulling and tugging at my space suit.

I tried to pull my leg out of the twisted line, but it was wrapped too tightly.

What a scorch! I thought.

I decided to unhook my line and try to untangle it myself.

As I squeezed open the catch, I looked over at Tad. He had the strangest look on his face. He began waving his hands frantically.

But it was too late.

My hand slipped, and I lost hold of the line!

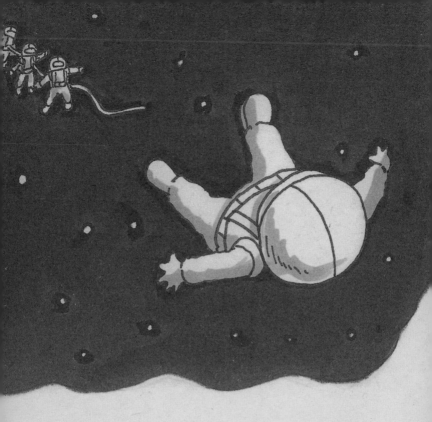

It spun me around and around, untwisting
my leg. When it let go, I was flung away from
my friends!

Slam! I thought as I drifted farther out into
space.

Space was a big place. I started to worry.
What if I drifted so far out, no one could find
me?

I fixed my eyes on my friends. Teena was closest to the space station. I watched as she quickly released the tether hold. It shot more line out to Tad, sending him closer to me.

Little by little, Tad inched toward me.

Ceedus-Lupeedus! I just hope there's enough tether line to reach me! I worried some more.

I had to stay calm. This was no time to go into global meltdown.

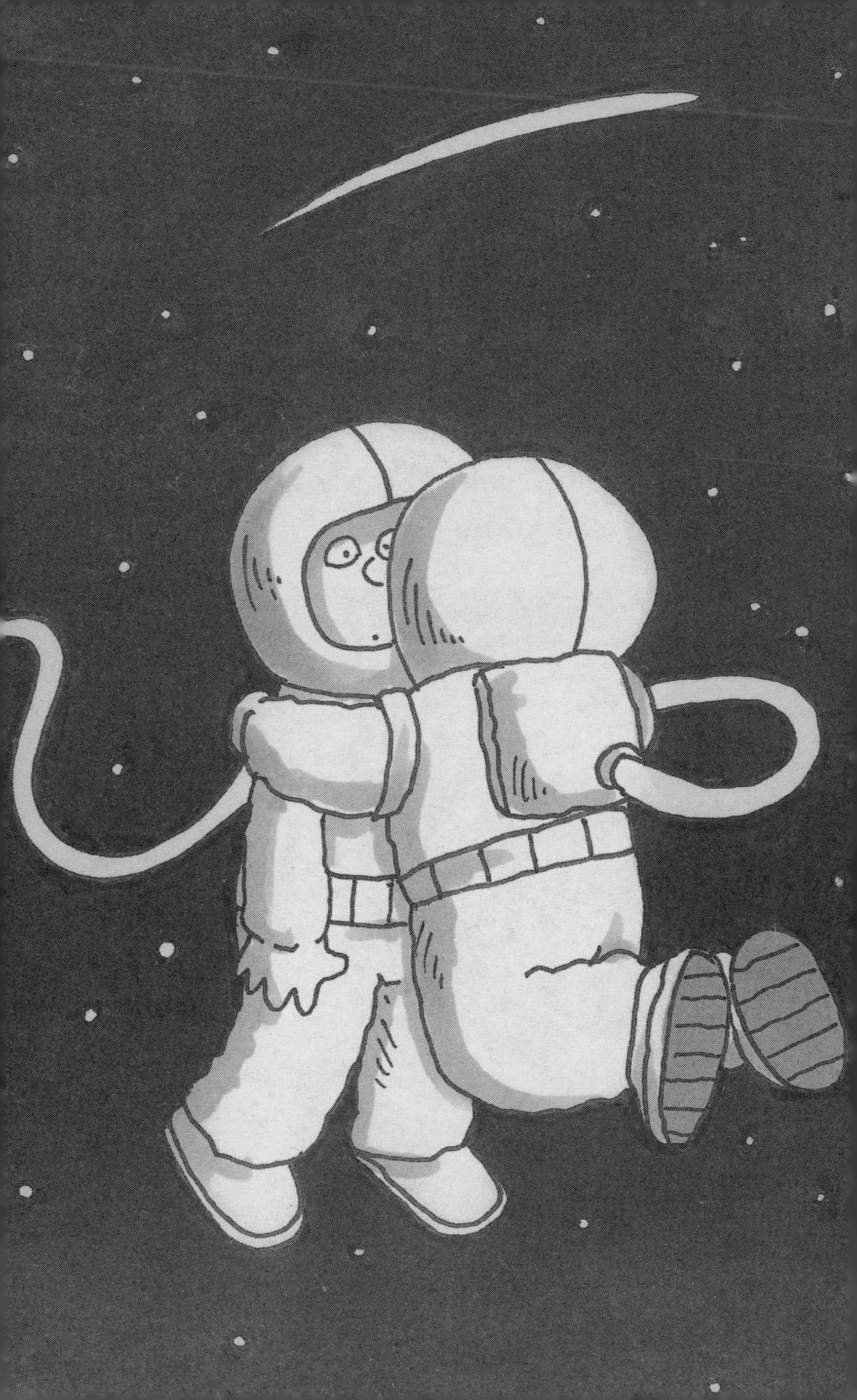

Finally, after what seemed like forever, Tad floated within a few feet of me.

With his outstretched hand, he grabbed hold of my sleeve. He pulled me in carefully. Then he hooked me back to the tether line.

I threw my arms around him. I was so happy to be saved. It was the most frightening thing that had ever happened to me.

From that moment on, I promised myself, I would never do anything scorchy again.

I did not feel much like spacewalking after that. My friends weren't having fun any longer, either. So we decided to return to the space station.

When we were back on board, my friends hugged me. I could tell they had been as scared as I had been.

We took off our space suits and hung them back on the wall. Then we slipped out the door of the exit deck.

"That was stellar!" said Teena, to my surprise, as she hopped onto my hoverboard.

My friends and I watched as Teena sped away like a comet on fire. When she reached the end of the hall, she couldn't make the turn.

She crashed into the space station wall. Sparks flew everywhere.

My friends and I looked at each other in disbelief.

Then the lights on the space station went out.

7
HIT-AND-RUN

My friends and I stood in the dark.

"She must have cut off the power when she hit the wall," said Tad.

Tad switched on his laser lamp. A beam of light shot down the hall.

Neb, Var, and I followed Tad to the crash site. When we reached it, Tad focused his light on the damaged wall. No one said anything while Tad's laser beam traveled back and forth across the broken circuits.

Finally, Tad spoke.

"Teena's really done it now," he said. "She's disrupted the kryzon connections and the flystroms are splitting!"

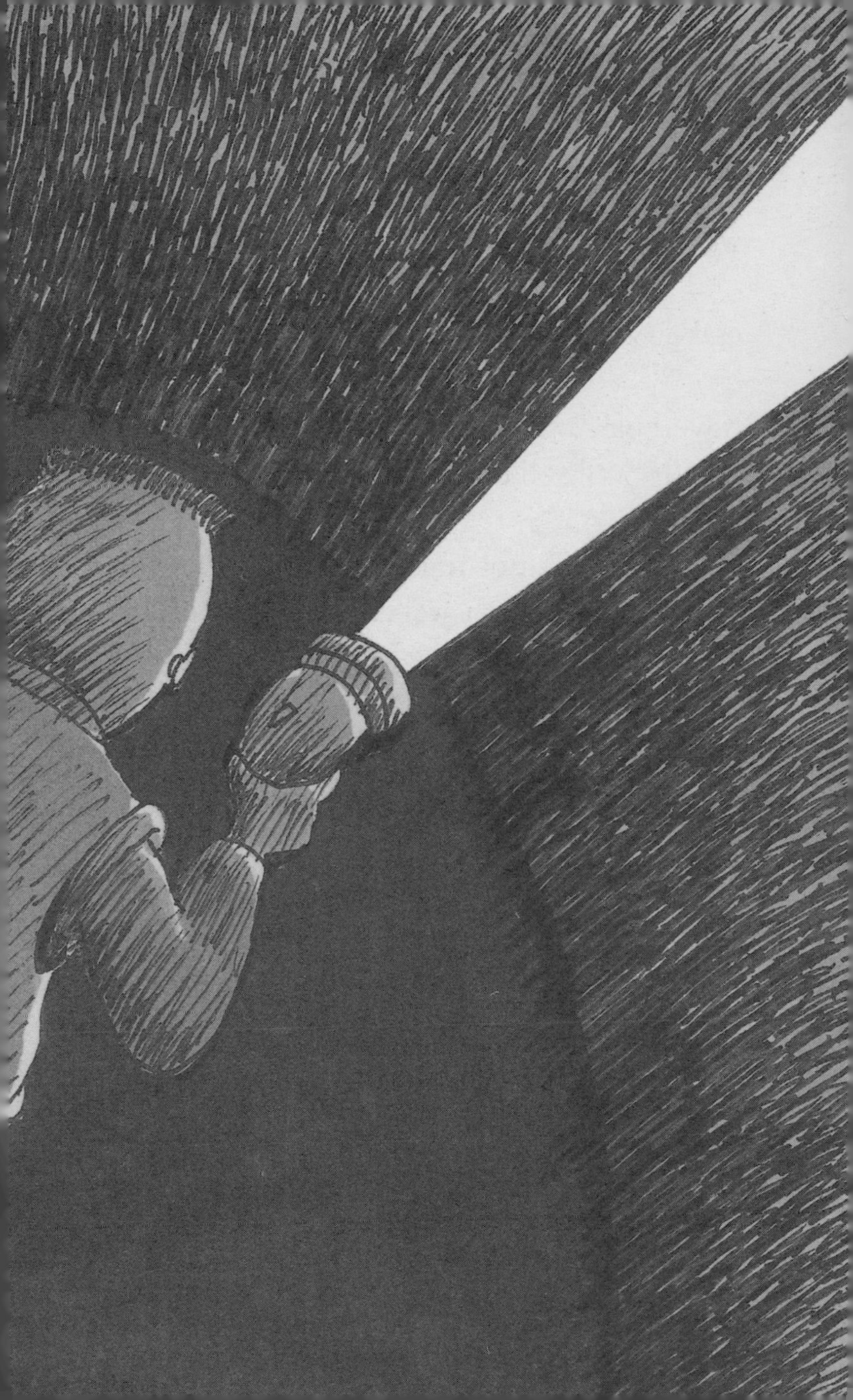

I looked over at Neb and Var. None of us knew what that meant. But if Tad thought it was scorchy, then we did, too.

"I wonder where Teena went, anyway?" asked Neb all of a sudden.

We looked down. Broken pieces of my hoverboard were scattered everywhere.

"It looks like a hit-and-run to me," said Var.

There was not much Tad could do without a kryzonometer, so we decided to go look for Teena.

My friends and I felt like we'd been swallowed up by a black hole. We did not understand how Teena could blast off and leave us in the dark.

We made our way down the hallways of Sector 7. By the time we reached Sector 6, the lights of the space station had come back on.

"That's just the backup power system," said Tad. "It will be a while before they repair the flystroms."

We looked everywhere for Teena. We

went to the Mars Malt. We stopped at the Big Wheel Shopping Mall. We even took the Q-Train back to Quantum Elementary.

"I haven't seen her," said Mr. Peres, looking up from a Fuddle-Frisson equation.

Finally, my friends and I got tired of looking for Teena. So we decided to go home.

"Data-pad me later!" I told them as I blasted off.

When I got home, my parents and Mr. Wiggins were watching the news on 3D-TV. They didn't look up when I came in. So I sat down on the sofa to watch with them.

What I heard next fully shivered me out.

"A broken hoverboard was found at the site of the crash that caused today's power outage," said the TV newscaster. "Captain Plank had this to say about the hit-and-run. . . ."

The camera switched to a close-up of a flared-up Captain Plank.

"I will not sleep until this criminal is found and punished!" he promised.

My dad turned off the 3D-TV. He was pretty flared-up, too.

"We have lost a whole day of work on our Fuddle-Frisson project because of that outlaw!" he told my mom.

"It's a shame," agreed Mr. Wiggins.

I slouched down on the sofa, trying to slide my way out of there. Then the door buzzer sounded.

A few moments later, Woma came into the living room.

"Captain Plank is here to see you, Zenon," she said.

I walked slowly across the room, my knees wobbly. My parents followed close behind me.

Captain Plank was standing in the doorway. He was holding a jagged piece of metal.

"Is this your hoverboard, Zenon Kar?" he asked me.

8
CRIME AND PUNISHMENT

I looked down at the jagged piece of metal in Captain Plank's hand.

"Yes . . . that's my hoverboard," I said to him slowly.

My parents and Mr. Wiggins gasped as they all turned and looked at me.

I was going to tell them what my hoverboard was doing at the crash site. But suddenly Teena walked in.

"Captain Plank!" she cried. "What a stellar surprise to see you!"

Teena looked down and saw the piece of my hoverboard in Captain Plank's hand. Then she turned and looked at me.

"Isn't that your hoverboard, Zenon?" she asked. "I know it split into a hundred pieces when you hit that wall!"

Ceedus-Lupeedus! I was so shivered out by her lie, I almost went into global meltdown!

"When *I* hit the wall?" I asked her.

I looked at Captain Plank. Then I looked at my parents and Mr. Wiggins. They were looking at me like I had done something wrong.

"*I* didn't hit the wall!" I shouted at them. "*Teena* hit the wall! *She* was riding my hoverboard!"

I could tell that no one believed me.

They were probably thinking, *How could a stellar girl like Teena Wiggins do a scorchy thing like that?*

"I am very disappointed in you, Zenon Kar," said Captain Plank.

"Your father and I will discuss your punishment later," said my mother.

I turned toward Teena and gave her the scorchiest look I could. Then I stormed out of the apartment and down the hall toward Nebula's place. The halls of the space station looked blurry through my teary eyes.

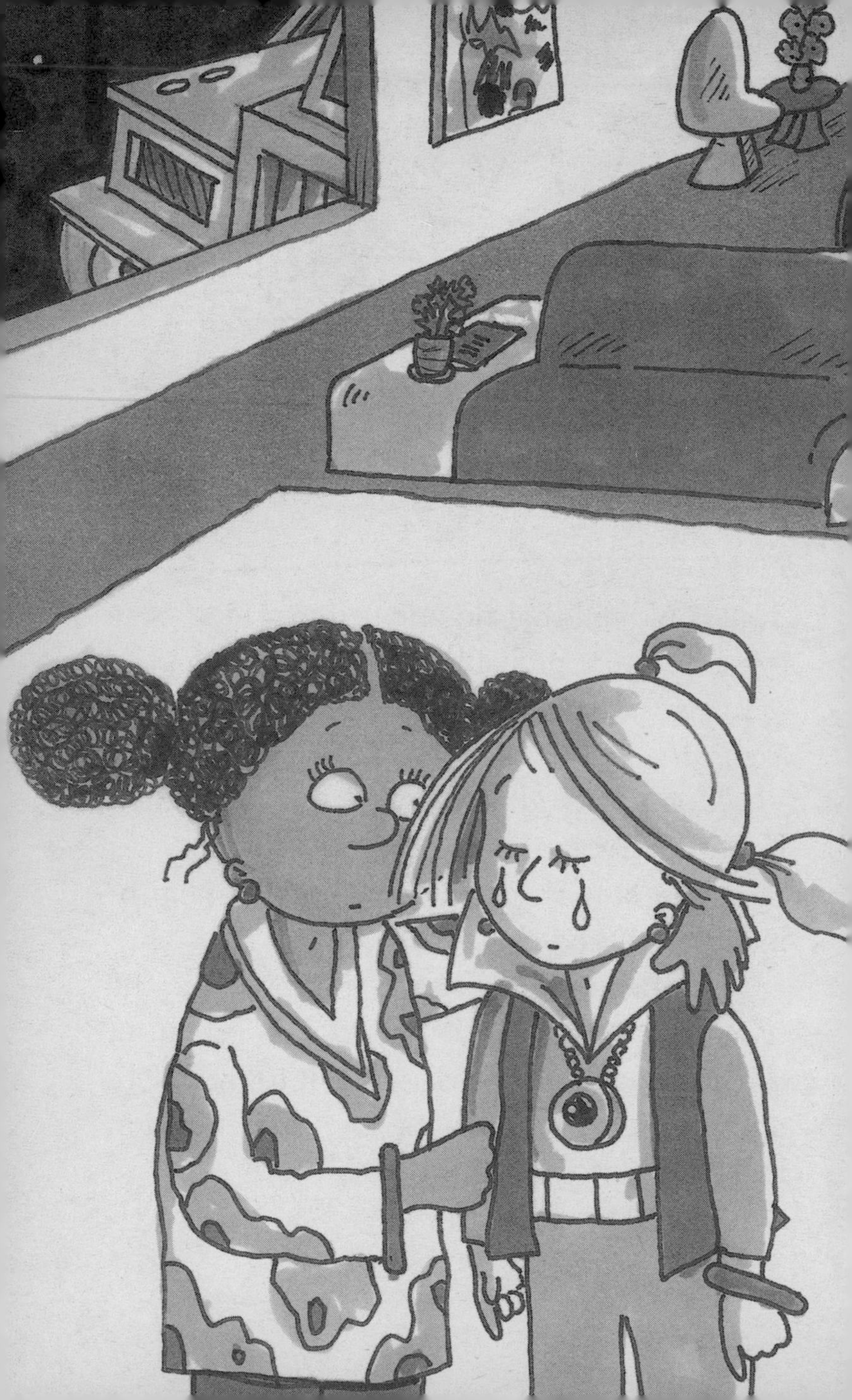

When I got to Nebula's, she was watching the news on 3D-TV. She had just seen the story about the crash.

"What a scorch!" she cried when she saw me. "Teena's in big trouble now!"

Then Nebula saw that I was crying.

"Oh, Zee! What's the matter?" she said, looking worried.

"Twee . . . na wied!" I said, sobbing.

Nebula threw her arms around me. And I explained everything that had happened. When I finished, Neb was so flared-up, her face looked like a Pandorian sunrise.

"I *knew* she was an alien!" she cried.

Nebula jumped up from her chair and started for the door.

"I'm going to talk to Captain Plank myself!" she shouted. "I'm a witness, Zee! I saw everything!"

Nebula wasn't thinking clearly. Her mind was in a Martian mist. I pulled her back into the room and sat her down.

"You're my best friend, Neb," I tried to

explain. "They'll never believe you, either."

Nebula and I sat quietly for a long time, thinking. It was not going to be easy to get out of this meltdown.

Then the most stellar thing happened.

"Where did you get that necklace?" asked Neb, pointing toward my neck. "I've never seen it before."

I looked down. It was the Alfred Geezle–designed Mini Motion-Picture Camera necklace that Teena had put around my neck! I had forgotten all about it!

"Ceedus-Lupeedus!" I shouted. "My problems may be over, Neb!"

9
A PICTURE WORTH A THOUSAND WORDS

I took off my necklace and showed it to Nebula. I told her Teena had given it to me. Then I explained what it *really* was and how it worked.

"If this camera recorded everything that happened over the last two days," I cried, "I will have the proof I need!"

I hooked up Teena's camera to Nebula's maxi-phone screen. Then I pushed the play button.

To my relief, the camera *had* been working!

Neb and I watched as two days in my life unfolded: Mr. Peres lecturing on Fuddlenomics . . . Teena meeting my friends for the first time . . . Captain Plank nearly being hit by my hoverboard . . . my friends drinking Whambama Shakes at the Mars Malt . . . then walking in space . . . and, finally, Teena speeding down the long hall in Sector 7 and crashing into the wall!

"Ceedus-Lupeedus! We've got her!" I cried, jumping out of my seat.

We couldn't wait to play the film for my parents, Mr. Wiggins, and Captain Plank. I grabbed the Mini Motion-Picture Camera necklace, and Neb and I dashed out the door.

When we got home, Teena and Mr. Wiggins were gone. But to my delight, Captain Plank was still there.

Discussing my punishment, no doubt, I thought.

Everyone looked at Neb and me with angry faces. I didn't give them a chance to say anything. I walked right over to our 3D-TV and hooked up Teena's Alfred Geezle–designed Mini Motion-Picture Camera.

"I have something to show you" was all I said.

Everyone quietly watched my film. When the recording was over, no one said anything for a moment. Then they all began to apologize.

"Zenon, I am very sorry," said Captain Plank. "I misjudged you."

"Me too," said my mom, giving me a hug. "It wasn't fair of us not to believe you."

I must admit, I was feeling smug. But I was still flared-up over what happened. And I was ready not to forgive any of them—for at least the next few days.

Then my dad spoke up.

"I'd like to see that film one more time," he said.

Everyone looked at him in surprise.

I didn't know why he wanted me to replay the film. But I could tell from the look on his face that I wasn't going to like it.

We watched again as Mr. Peres lectured . . . as Teena met my friends . . . as Captain Plank was nearly hit . . . as we drank Whambama Shakes . . . as . . . Ceedus-Lupeedus! There it was! The spacewalk! I'd forgotten all about the spacewalk!

"Now tell me about *this* part of your film," my dad said as he paused the camera.

All eyes turned toward me as I slumped forward in my seat like a Blotozoid Zombie.

"It wasn't *my* idea . . . ," I started to say.

Then I stopped and looked around at everyone.

I wanted to tell them that it had been *Teena's* idea to go on a spacewalk. *She* was the one who had turned down the hall at Sector 7. *She* was the one who had picked the lock with her little black box. *She* was the one who had opened the door to outer space.

But I just couldn't do it.

I didn't want to be like Teena anymore, not if it meant blaming someone else for my own scorchy behavior.

"I'm sorry," I said. "I went on a spacewalk even though I knew I wasn't allowed. I have no one to blame but myself."

Mom and Dad looked at me for a long time without saying anything. Then they both gave me a hug.

"We're proud of you, honey, for telling the truth," they said.

I was feeling pretty thermo about myself. In fact, I was feeling pretty thermo about everything.

Then Teena walked back into the room.

10
THE TROUBLE
WITH TEENA

Teena saw her Mini Motion-Picture Camera necklace hooked up to the 3D-TV. Then she turned and looked around the room at us. She knew right away what had happened.

Teena did not say anything. She did not go lunar. She did not go into global meltdown.

She was as cool as a Milky Way Float.

Captain Plank had plenty to say, however.

"I will be grounding you, Teena Wiggins," he said, pointing to Earth outside the space station window. "You will be leaving on the first shuttle out in the morning."

On his way out the door, Captain Plank wished my dad and Mr. Wiggins good luck on their Fuddle-Frisson project.

Mr. Wiggins decided to stay on the space station for a few days longer. He would not be leaving in the morning with his daughter, he said. He was far too close to a solution for the Fuddle-Frisson project.

No one said anything else about the hit-and-run crash. No one said anything else about Teena's lie.

When it was time for dinner, Woma called us into the kitchen. She had fixed beet kabobs for Teena's last supper.

That night, Teena and I went to bed early.
I gazed out at the stars while Teena fell asleep.

*How can she sleep so peacefully after all the
trouble she caused?* I wondered.

Bobo curled up next to me in bed.

"Teena go home?" he asked.

"Yes, Bobo," I said. "Teena go home in the
morning. Thank goodness."

Then I fell asleep with Bobo in my arms.

The next morning, Teena and I ate breakfast together. We did not have time for Pandorian toast, so we had cereal instead.

"What will you do when you get home?" I asked.

Teena looked up from her bowl of Snackle Frax, grinning from ear to ear.

"I'll blast off to Ground Hogs to see my friends!" she said happily.

Then she went back to eating her cereal.

I wanted to tell Teena that there were more important things in life than having fun.

You can't go through life like a Freefron! I thought.

But I didn't think Teena would listen. I could only hope her father would find the time to tell her before she ended up in a truly serious global meltdown.

When it was time to leave for the shuttle port, Dad carried Teena's bags to the train stop. Teena practically danced down the hallway.

Grounding was the worst thing I could think of that could happen to me. But Teena was acting like she couldn't wait to get back to Earth. Like she was getting exactly what she wanted.

The shuttle was right on time. Mr. Wiggins hugged his daughter goodbye. Then my mom and dad hugged her as well.

Teena and I stood alone on the departure deck for a moment. As I said goodbye, I handed her the Alfred Geezle–designed Mini Motion-Picture Camera necklace.

"Thanks for letting me wear it," I said. "I found it very useful."

Teena shrugged as she took the necklace and put it around her neck.

"Goodbye, Zenon," she said with a smile. Then she winked and said, "Stay out of trouble!"

I watched her turn and run up the shuttle stairs. She seemed to be laughing in the window as the shuttle lifted off.

A few moments later, the lights on the space station went out.

I had two thoughts:

How in the name of Neptune did she do it?

And who in the name of Pluto was she going to blame this time?

11
ZENON'S GUIDE TO SPACE STATION SLANG

These are some of the terms you'll hear when you visit me on Space Station 9:

Alfred Geezle
He is a 21st-century designer of everything from the clocks on our walls to the treads on our shoes.

beet loaf, beetballs, beetburger, beet kabobs
Beets, as you may have guessed, are the main ingredient in these delicious dishes on Space Station 9!

Blanchy
See Plutar Blanchy.

Blotozoid Freefron
This is a character from one of the scariest movies I have ever seen, *The Night of the Blotozoid Zombies!* It is a nervous, skinny creature that can never sit still and is always on the go.

Blotozoid Zombie
This character is also from the *Blotozoid Zombies* movie (mentioned above). It is a very pale creature that slumps forward when it walks. Yuck!

Ceedus-Lupeedus!
This is our favorite thing to say when we are surprised by something we see or hear.

chill chamber
This is a place, like the Mars Malt, where we go to relax.

cool your boosters
This means you need to calm down.

data pads
These are our portable computers.

Fenebula
This is the most distant galaxy our
scientists have been able to identify.

flared-up
You're flared-up when you're upset and angry
and your face turns as red as a solar flare.

flystrom
You will find this small piece of computer
equipment inside most of our robots and
machines. It's part of what makes them work.
If you need to know more, you'll have to ask
my dad.

Freefron
See Blotozoid Freefron.

Fuddle-Frisson
This is a form of energy that is so confusing, it leaves almost everyone befuddled.

Fuddlenomics
This is the study of Fuddle-Frisson. It is one of my hardest subjects in school.

geezle bumps
Although these are like goose bumps, we call them geezle bumps. They look like the treads on the bottoms of the shoes we wear, which were designed by Alfred Geezle.

global meltdown
You go into this when you get upset and lose control of yourself.

grounding
A space station punishment that sends you down to Earth for a period of time.

kryzon
This is the largest working part of a flystrom.

kryzonometer
This is a device that measures the speed at which a kryzon turns.

Laser Frissonometer
This is a tool that measures Fuddle-Frisson energy with a laser beam.

Lootar
See Pandorian Lootar.

lunar
(as in "going lunar")
This is the same as going crazy.

Martian mist
When your mind is kind of foggy and con-fused, you're in a Martian mist.

Pandorian Lootar
This is a huge monster in a 3-D video game that we love to play.

Pandorian toast
This is toast fixed dark and crispy on the outside, soft and buttery on the inside. Woma's is the best and she isn't even Pandorian!

Plutar Blanchy
This is a character from one of my favorite children's books, *It's Not Easy Being a Plutar Blanchy*. It is a goofy, easily frightened creature that walks around grinning.

quasar
When someone goes quasar, like my dad, it means that he is very excited because something has made him happy.

scorch
When something is a scorch or scorchy, it's a bad, bad thing.

shivered out
(or "shiver me out")
You get this way when something or someone really gives you the creeps.

Snackle Frax
My favorite breakfast cereal. *Snacklefrax* is the sound it makes when you pour milk on it.

solar mist
This is the hazy mist that seems to surround anything that is backlit by the sun.

stellar
If something is stellar, it is the most wonderful thing you can imagine!